ALICE OSEMAN

NICK AND CHARLIE
THIS WINTER
RADIO SILENCE
LOVELESS
HEARTSTOPPER
I WAS BORN FOR THIS
SOLITAIRE
HEARTSTOPPER

Books by Alice Oseman

SOLITAIRE

RADIO SILENCE

I WAS BORN FOR THIS

LOVELESS

WINNER OF THE YA BOOK PRIZE 2021

Novellas by Alice Oseman

NICK AND CHARLIE

THIS WINTER

Graphic Novels by Alice Oseman

HEARTSTOPPER VOLUME 1

HEARTSTOPPER VOLUME 2

HEARTSTOPPER VOLUME 3

HEARTSTOPPER VOLUME 4

hi
SNAP

'Yes, very indifferent indeed,' said Elizabeth, laughingly. 'Oh, Jane, take care.'

'My dear Lizzy, you cannot think me so weak, as to be in danger now?'

'I think you are in very great danger of making him as much in love with you as ever.'

Pride and Prejudice, Jane Austen

ONE

Charlie

As Head Boy of Truham Grammar School, I've done many things. I got drunk on the wine at parents' evening. I've been photographed with the mayor three times. I once accidentally made a Year 7 cry.

But none of that was quite as bad as having to stop everyone in Year 13 from enjoying their final day of school, which is what our head teacher, Mr Shannon, is trying to make me do right now.

It's probably worth mentioning that my boyfriend of two years, Nick Nelson, is one of those Year 13s.

'You don't mind, do you?' Mr Shannon leans on the common-room table where I'm supposed to be revising for my exams but am actually watching Mac DeMarco concerts on my phone. 'It's all got a bit out of hand and I think they'd be more likely to listen to you than me, if you see what I mean.'

'Erm . . .' I shoot a look at my friend Tao Xu who's sitting next to me eating a packet of Galaxy Minstrels. He raises his eyebrows at me as if to say, 'Sucks to be you'.

I don't really want to say yes.

Year 13's final day of school is *High School Musical* themed. They've hung a giant 'East High' sign over the Truham one at the school gate. They've been playing the soundtrack on classroom computers, so wherever you are in the school you can hear a *High School Musical* song playing from somewhere, but you're never quite sure where. They participated in a 'What Time Is It' flash mob on the football field at breaktime. And they have all turned up to school either in red basketball outfits or cheerleader outfits. Disappointingly, Nick went for basketballer.

To top it all off, on a non-*HSM*-related note, they've built a fort out of cardboard boxes on the tennis courts and are having a barbeque inside it.

'I just want them to put the barbeque out,' says Shannon, obviously detecting how reluctant I am to walk into a box fort of one hundred and fifty people older than me and tell them to stop having fun. 'You know. Health and safety stuff. If someone gets burnt, I'll be the one dealing with angry parents.'

He chuckles. Mr Shannon has come to trust me completely over the several months I have been Head Boy. This is hilarious because I rarely do anything he tells me to do.

Keep the teachers on your side and the students on your side. Don't make enemies or too many friends.

That's my advice for getting through school.

'Yeah, sure, no problem,' I say.

'You're an absolute life saver.' He points a finger at me as he walks away. 'Don't revise too hard!'

Tao looks at me, still shoving chocolate into his mouth. 'You're not actually gonna go confront the Year 13s, are you?'

I laugh. 'Nah. I'll just go see what they're up to and tell them to watch out for Shannon.'

My other friend, Aled Last, looks up at me from the opposite side of the table. He's been colour-coding his maths revision notes for the past hour. 'Can you bring me back a burger?'

I stand up from my chair and put my blazer on. 'If there's any left.'

The Year 12s have already left for study leave and the only reason I'm here is because I revise better at school than at home. Tao and Aled thought the same.

None of us really want to be here though. It's the hottest day we've had this year and I just sort of want to lie down somewhere with an ice pack on my head.

Nick and I have plans for this weekend. He's finally free from school, I'm taking a weekend off revision. It's Thursday today; I'm staying over his tonight. Tomorrow night we're going to Harry's party for everyone in sixth form. Saturday we're going to the beach. Sunday we're going to London.

Not that we don't spend every weekend together anyway.

Not that we don't see each other every single day.

If you'd told me three years ago I'd be in a two-year-long relationship by the time I was seventeen, I would have laughed in your face.

'CHARLIE SPRING!'

As I walk through the box-fort entrance underneath a banner that says 'WILDCATS!' Harry Greene approaches me, arms outstretched. He is wearing a twelve-year-old's *High School Musical* cheerleader costume and is exposing a lot more thigh than is probably appropriate for school.

The fort is huge – they've taken over two tennis courts. Along with the hilarious amount of cardboard, they've also stolen at least ten tables from various classrooms and have a fully functioning barbeque set up in between the two courts. A couple of people are handing out burgers and buns. Vampire Weekend is playing from a wireless speaker in a corner.

Most, if not all, of Year 13 are here. It's a *huge* year group compared to the rest of the school – a lot of the Higgs girls from that year group moved to Truham after there was a big fire at Higgs and a few buildings burned down. Long story.

Harry puts his hands on his hips and grins up at me. 'Thoughts?'

Harry Greene, a fairly short guy with very tall hair,

is probably the most notorious individual in the entire school, partly due to how many parties he throws and partly due to the fact that he never, ever shuts up.

I raise my eyebrows. 'About the fort or about your thighs?'

'Both, mate.'

'Both are great,' I say, deadpan. 'Good job. Keep it up.'

Harry steps to one side and lunges. 'I knew the skirt was a good decision. I should do this more often.'

'Definitely.'

Harry used to be a pretty nasty person – just one of the many older boys who gave me shit when I was younger and the only out kid in school. But over the years, thankfully, he's gotten over himself and realised that being homophobic isn't cool. Not that I've forgiven him, though. Nick and I still think he's a massive knob.

Still in a lunging position, he asks, 'Did Shannon send you? Have you come to shut down our fun?'

'Technically, yes.'

'Are you going to?'

'Obviously not.'

Harry nods. 'You're gonna go far, mate. You're gonna go far.'

Nick is usually very easy to spot in a crowd, but today almost everyone is wearing red. There are a few people who clearly couldn't be bothered, one being my sister Tori, who's in her black Truham uniform, sitting on the blue asphalt in a corner talking to her friend Rita. But apart from her and a couple of others, everyone blurs into one giant mass of red.

'Nick's over there.'

I look back at Harry and he's pointing towards the far left corner, grinning at me. Then he starts walking towards the corner, humming 'We're All in This Together', and I follow him.

'NICK, MATE!' Harry shouts over the crowds of

Year 13s, all holding food and red plastic cups and taking photos of each other.

And there he is.

He turns round from a small group of people, a slightly dazed expression on his face as if he's not quite sure whether he's imagining Harry's voice.

I have been going out with Nick Nelson since I was fourteen. He likes rugby and Formula 1, animals (especially dogs), the Marvel universe, the sound felt-tips make on paper, rain, drawing on shoes, Disneyland and minimalism. He also likes me.

His hair is dark blond and his eyes are brown and he is two inches taller than me, if you care about that sort of thing. I think he's pretty hot, but that might just be my opinion.

When he spots us, he waves enthusiastically, and when we finally reach him, he looks at me and says, 'All right?'

Nick's *High School Musical* costume consists of a pair of bright red gym shorts and a red tank top. He's pinned a piece of paper to the front with a very badly drawn wildcat on it. If I'm honest, he's had worse outfits.

'You didn't text me back,' I say.

He sips his drink. 'I was way too busy getting my head in the game.'

Then he holds up a disposable camera and, before I have the chance to smile or make sure I look in any way presentable, takes a photo of me.

A second too late I hold up my hand in front of the camera. 'Nick!'

He lets out a loud laugh and starts rewinding the camera before putting it in his pocket. 'Another one for the Derp Charlie collection.'

'Oh my god.'

Harry's already wandered off to talk to another group, so Nick steps a little closer and our hands automatically touch, his tapping mine like we're playing a clapping game. 'You sticking round here for a bit? Or are you revising?'

I glance round. 'I wasn't really revising. I was watching Mac DeMarco concerts.'

'Ah. Of course.'

We just sort of stand there for a bit, hands touching, and then Nick brings up a hand to adjust my hair slightly. It hits me suddenly that this is the last day we're going to be at the same school. Six entire years of being in the same place every weekday are over. The two years we've been a couple at school, two years of eating lunch together, sitting in form, hiding in music rooms, I.T. rooms, P.E. changing rooms, two years of going home together, walking when it's sunny, getting the bus when it's cold, Nick drawing faces in the window condensation, me falling asleep on his shoulder. It's all over.

Normally we talk about this stuff – stuff that we

get sad about or annoyed about or angry about – but Nick's really excited about uni so I don't want to start complaining or make him feel bad. I've done more than enough of that in my life, for God's sake. I just . . . I'm the one getting left behind, which is kind of crap, really.

We look up when we hear a small 'click' and a loud laugh. We turn and Harry is holding Nick's camera up to us gleefully. 'So bloody romantic. I can't believe I'm gonna have to find a new couple to cockblock at uni.'

Nick snatches the camera back. 'Did you literally just pickpocket me?'

Harry winks and laughs at him before wandering away again. Nick shakes his head and rewinds the camera. 'God, he's so *irritating*.'

'Where'd you get the camera from?'

'I bought it. I thought it'd be good to have some actual physical photos to put on my uni wall instead of just crappy photos on my phone.'

I grab it out of his hands and take a picture of him.

'Hey!' He grabs it back, grinning. 'I don't want pictures of just *me*. Everyone'll think I'm obsessed with myself.'

I smile too. 'I'll have that one then.'

Nick puts his arm around me. 'Okay, we need at least one picture together where we look fucking *normal*.' He holds the camera up in front of us, the lens facing us, and I say, 'Let's be honest, we never look normal,' and Nick laughs at me while I'm making sure my hair isn't doing something weird, and then we both smile, and he takes the picture.

'When I visit you at uni, I'm expecting that one framed,' I say.

'Only if you buy me a frame. I'll have rent to pay.'

'God, get a job.'

'What? You mean you're not going to buy me things now that you have a job? I can't believe this. Why am I even in this relationship?'

'I don't even know, Nick. Why are you still here? It's been over two years.'

Nick just laughs and kisses me quickly on the cheek, then starts to walk backwards away towards the drinks table. 'You're nice to look at.'

I give him the middle finger.

When we first started going out, we didn't tell people for a while. We didn't really know how people would react to us, so it was safer to just be low-key. There hadn't been an openly gay couple in our school, well, *ever*, as far as we knew, and I'd been bullied a lot when I was outed. So we didn't hold hands. We didn't flirt when other people were around. Sometimes I even felt kind of awkward just *talking* to him in school, just in case someone found out, and started bullying me again, or worse, started bullying *Nick* too.

Nowadays, we don't have to be scared here. I hold his hand whenever I want.

Nick

So I might've cried when the final bell went. Just a little bit.

I wasn't as bad as Harry. He was bawling his eyes out and hugging everyone, including some scared-looking Year 7s who just wanted to catch their bus.

Even though it's not like today was the last time I'll ever see my friends, it still feels sad. Never wearing our uniforms again, no more lunchtime rounders on the field, the end of Wednesday period-five biscuit hour in the common room.

No more hanging out with Charlie at school.

I guess there are a few things I'm a bit nervous about. Coming out as bisexual again is probably the main one – I mean, I have to come out to someone every other day anyway, but new uni friends means a new load of people who are probably going to assume I'm straight. Leaving home's gonna be scary too. I'm a bit worried about my mum being by herself all the time.

And, again, there's leaving Charlie behind.

Still, there are loads of good things about leaving school – *God*, I'm ready for university, for doing my own thing whenever I want, for actually learning stuff I'm *interested* in. Finally getting out of this dingy town, having my own place, buying my own food, choosing how to spend my time.

It's scary. And I'll miss a lot of things. But I'm ready to go.

'Harry wants to know whether we'll be at his leavers' party tomorrow,' Charlie says from the passenger seat of my car, scrolling through something on his phone. People we know usually message Charlie these days when they want to talk to either of us because I'm horrific at replying to messages. He's way more organised than me.

'Well, I'm still up for it if you are,' I say, turning the car out of the school car park.

'Yeah, we should probably go, since prom's going to be crap.'

'Fair.'

We sit in comfortable silence as I drive us to my house. Charlie picks up his sunglasses from the door compartment and puts them on, then turns the radio on and continues scrolling through his phone, probably through Tumblr, his knees bent and his feet on the seat. Honestly, it's a beautiful day. Blue skies all round, reflecting off town windows and cars. I roll my window down and turn up the radio, and then

I take my disposable camera out of my pocket and quickly take a picture of Charlie, his face all sunlit, his dark hair being blown about by the wind, his body curled up on the passenger seat.

He looks at me instantly, but he's smiling. '*Nick*!'

I grin and look back at the road. 'Don't mind me.'

'At least give me some warning.'

'That's not as fun.'

This is normal for us, going to one of our houses after school. We spend more time at my house, generally. As my mum's usually at work and my brother's got his own place now, we have the house to ourselves. Over the past few months, our parents have been letting us stay over each other's houses sometimes, even on school nights. My mum never minds, but Charlie's parents are stricter and Charlie thinks that if he asked more than a couple of times a week, they'd start saying no.

We get that this isn't, like, *normal* normal. We think our parents see it's not normal as well. I mean, don't get me wrong, they're fine with it, but . . . normal teenage couples don't sleep round each other's houses on school nights, do they? They don't spend every single day with each other, right? I don't know.

We don't care.

★

Things me and Charlie do together at our houses include:

Play video games. Watch TV and films. Watch YouTube videos. Homework. Coursework. Revision. Nap. Make out. Have sex. Sit in the same room on different laptops in silence. Play board games. Make food. Make drinks. Get drunk. Plan trips to concerts. Plan holidays. Build pillow forts. Have sex in a pillow fort (okay, it was only once, but it did happen, I swear). Play with my dogs, Henry and Nellie. Help

KISS
KISS
BORK
BORK
GLUG
GLUG
TAP
TAP
TAP
Z
Z
Z

Charlie's brother, Oliver, with various Lego projects. Talk. Argue. Shout. Cry. Laugh. Cuddle. Sleep. Text each other from different rooms. Charlie practises his drums, makes playlists, reads books. I take photos on my phone, draw on Charlie when he's not looking, make meals neither of us has tried before.

We're pretty chill. Maybe kind of boring. But, in all honesty, that's fine with both of us.

Today's nothing different. We get in, we get drinks, I change into some jogging bottoms and a sweatshirt. Charlie changes into some jeans and a T-shirt he left here yesterday, and then collapses on to my bed, stretches out on his stomach and opens my laptop.

'D'you want any food?' I ask as I'm about to go downstairs.

I always ask him this after school. Charlie had anorexia pretty badly the year we started going out. He had to go to a psychiatric hospital for a couple of months and it really helped, but I guess he still sort of has it. Stuff like that doesn't go away very quickly. But he's nowhere near as bad as he used to be and he's better in lots of other ways too. He's usually fine with main meals now, even if he doesn't eat snacks, like, ever.

'Nah, I'm good,' he says, as usual.

I always make sure to ask though. I think he might say yes one day, if I just keep asking.

Once I've made my way through two slices of toast and a glass of lemonade, I come back upstairs to find Charlie frowning at the laptop screen.

I fall on to my bed next to him. 'What's up?'

He glances at me and then back at the laptop before clicking on something. 'Nothing. Just reading something on Tumblr.'

I don't have Tumblr, despite Charlie trying to make me use it many times. I don't really think it's my sort of thing.

Charlie rolls on to his back to make room for me and

takes out his phone. I lie down next to him and pull the laptop towards me. He's already exited Tumblr, so it probably wasn't anything I would have been interested in.

On another tab is the page I started reading this morning about the University of Leeds' rugby team, which I'm gonna try and join when I get there, if I'm good enough.

That's where I'm going in September – the University of Leeds. It's pretty far away; like, two hundred miles or something, and me and Charlie have obviously talked about the fact that we'll be long distance. While it's not ideal and nowhere near as great as the way we hang out every day at the moment, we're both completely fine with it. Charlie has a part-time job at a café now, so he reckons he can get the train to see me every few weeks, and I can get the train back every few weeks, and that means we'll definitely see each other at least every two weeks, if not more. And we'll text and call and Facetime loads anyway.

I start telling Charlie all the facts about Leeds' rugby team – how many tiers there are at the university and whether I think I'll be able to get in (I honestly do, I mean, I'm pretty good at rugby, in my opinion), how much their gym membership is and whether I'll be able to get a job somewhere when I get there, whether it's worth trying to get a sports scholarship, whether I'll be really crap compared to everyone else, and how nice their uniform is (green and white).

Charlie stays still on his back and listens and asks a few questions, but after I've been rambling on for a while I can tell he's getting bored because his voice quietens and he starts fiddling with my sweatshirt sleeve, and then, as I'm in the middle of a sentence, he rolls on to his side and pulls me down by the back of my neck for a kiss, which sort of takes me by surprise because we're long past the stage of needing to make out every time we're alone.

After a few seconds I go to move backwards, but he just pulls me further down. I laugh against his lips and I feel him smile too, but neither of us stop and after a minute or so I feel my hand subconsciously reach to run through his hair. This is a bit of an odd time of day for us to be doing this, but it's difficult to care, especially when he surges forward so he's lying on top of me.

'Did you want to talk about something else?' I murmur, wondering where this has come from. I push his hair back from his forehead. I probably have a thing for Charlie's hair.

He meets my eyes. Then he sits up, leans back and switches on the radio. The Vaccines are playing. He moves back down, tilts his head and says, 'Not really,' and then his lips are on mine.

Charlie

Basically, I hate hearing Nick talk about university.

I'm a horrible person.

He's ridiculously excited about going to uni. And he should be. I'm glad he is.

But lately he's been talking about it *all of the time.* And every single time he mentions it, it just reminds me that we're approaching the end of this. That come September, I'm getting left behind.

Basically, I'm scared.

People keep messaging me on Tumblr about it too

and they haven't been helping. I've got quite a lot of followers on Tumblr and many of them are interested in Nick and me. Like, *really* interested. It's a little creepy, actually.

So as soon as I mentioned that we'd be long distance from September, I was *flooded* with Tumblr asks about how I should be prepared for all the horrible things that come with long-distance relationships. And they're pissing me off. I stopped answering them a couple of days ago, but people are still sending them. I don't even understand why all these people care that much to make the effort to send me messages about it.

Thankfully, Nick doesn't mention university for the rest of the day, not when we take his dogs for a walk, not during dinner, not while we're watching *Alien*. When he wanders off to have a shower at around ten o'clock, I check my Tumblr inbox again, and there are even *more* now.

Anonymous said:

Have you talked to Nick about what it's gonna be like when he goes away? I know so many couples that tried to make it work when one of them went to uni and they all ended up breaking up. You should really at least talk to him about it.

Anonymous said:

isn't it weird u've been together so long tho??? like 14 is so young to get into a relationship. u shouldn't feel like u have to stay in ur first relationship forever . . .

Anonymous said:

Dude long distance never works, trust me it's better to end it now and save yourself the pain

Anonymous said:

Everyone should go into uni single!! University years are your sexiest years!! Gotta bang as many people as you can!!!!

I don't really want to bring this up with Nick because I don't want him to feel *bad* for going to university. He's completely right to be excited about it.

It doesn't matter how I feel about it.

Nick returns from the bathroom in just pyjama shorts, rubbing a towel over his hair. 'What's up?'

'What?'

'You're frowning again.'

I quickly close the Tumblr app. 'Am I?'

He walks over to the mirror and picks up his hairdryer. 'Yep.'

'Maybe that's just my face.'

'Nah, your face is usually way nicer.'

I hurl a pillow in his direction, but he steps to one side to dodge it, laughing.

I can't tell him about this. He'd feel awful. He's had enough of feeling bad because of me. I've already been the most annoying boyfriend in recorded history, what with all my mental health stuff.

'Come take a selfie with me,' I say. 'I want to piss off my Tumblr followers.'

Nick grins and puts down the hairdryer. 'Why would that piss them off?'

'Selfies piss everyone off.'

'So passive aggressive.' He walks over to the bed and flops down next to me.

I open the camera on my phone and before he has the chance to say anything about it, I kiss him on the cheek and take the photo like that.

Nick laughs again. 'Oh, you're doing that on the Internet now, are you?'

SNAP

I wrap my arms around him. 'You know it's what they all want.'

'At least let me sort out my hair.'

'It looks good when it's wet.'

We lean our heads together and I make a peace sign with one hand and take another picture. Then I take one of us actually kissing, but I don't put that one on Tumblr. Some things are nicer if they're just for us.

Nick

The next morning I wake up to the sound of Charlie's phone alarm – he always sets it to an annoying un-ignorable beeping sound rather than music like I do. Despite this, waking up next to Charlie is definitely better than any other way of waking up. I don't really know why. My bed always feels sort of cold when he's not there.

Charlie's still insisting he has to go to school today because he's bad at revising at home, so he's making me get up at seven o'clock in the morning to drive him. While I could go to school to revise, the idea of trying to revise on the first day of my study leave kind of makes me want to burn all of my revision notes, and also we're both crap at doing schoolwork when we're together anyway.

I open my eyes to see him stirring. A line of sunshine falls across his chest through the gap in the curtains, and even while I'm still half-asleep I get another sudden urge to take a picture of him. Then I remember that I already took one of him asleep last night anyway, when I found him curled up in my bed after I'd gone to get a glass of water, and that had used up the camera film.

Charlie rolls over to turn off the alarm and then goes to climb over me to get out of bed – my bed's situated against the wall – but as he does I slide my hands round his waist and pull him down on top of me. He lets out a surprised noise and then a small laugh, his voice still sleepy. 'I have to go shower—'

'No, stay here.'

'I can't, I'll fall asleep again.'

'Don't go to school.'

'Nick!'

'Stay here with me.'

'I can't, I've got to . . . I need to revise.'

'Mm, fine.' I loosen my arms so Charlie can wrestle himself out of them. As soon as he's gone, my bed feels cold and empty again. It's pretty dumb, really. I sleep alone most of the time.

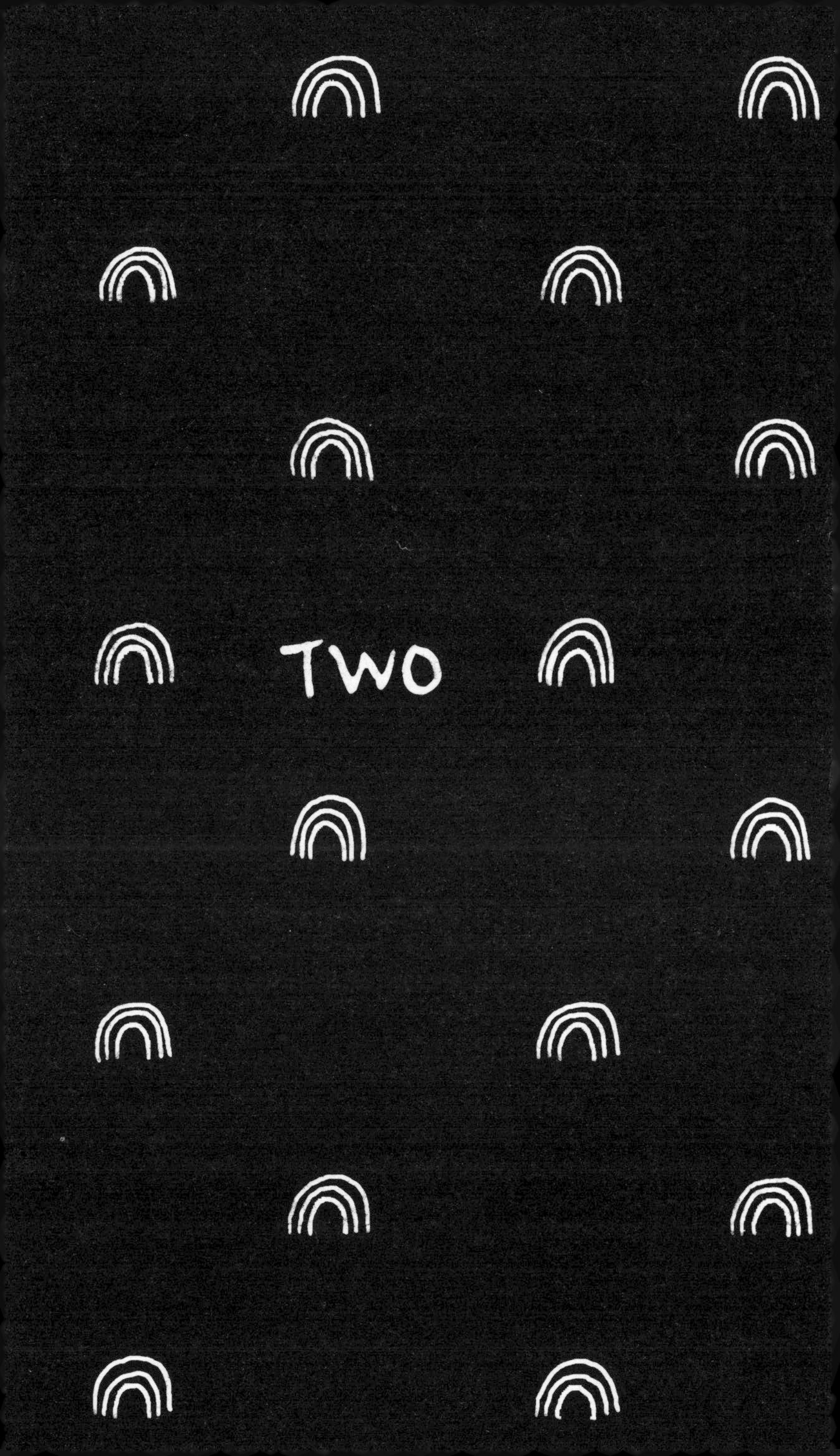
TWO

Charlie

I sort of hoped Nick might have picked up on how I've been feeling. Normally he's pretty good at that; like, *weirdly* good, actually. And I'm not exactly subtle in my attempts to get him to stop talking about uni. But by third period, after I text Nick to see whether he's awake again (after dropping me off at school, he said he was going back to bed), the excited text onslaught begins.

Nick Nelson

(11:34) *We should go uni shopping soon!!! Is it weird I'm excited about buying kitchen utensils?*

Nick Nelson

(12:02) *Dyou think I should email to check whether I'll have a double bed?? Like how do people know which sheets to buy?*

(12:05) *I'd better have a double bed lol your bed is bad enough*

Nick Nelson

(12:46) *Dyou think I should take my xbox or is that too unsociable? I need people to like me*

Nick Nelson

(12:54) *Is Kaleem in school?? If he is can you ask him whether he knows about the beds?*

Nick Nelson

(13:15) *I'm way more interested in home furnishing than I thought. The ikea website is a dangerous vortex*

I reply to all his messages and really try to be enthusiastic, but I can tell my texts sound a bit flat. Nick doesn't seem to notice though. He just keeps texting me about university and buying stuff for his room and the modules he thinks he wants to take and all sorts of other things that just make me feel increasingly awful by the second.

We've talked about it before. Quite a while ago actually, back when Nick was looking round universities last summer and when he was applying to them in the autumn. I admitted I was pretty worried about him leaving. I said I was scared of being on my own all the time. It was kind of embarrassing, really. Stupid. *Scared of being on my own.* I sounded like I was three years old.

Nick obviously reassured me we'd talk all the time anyway and everything would be fine. We haven't talked about it much since then, but only because there's not much more to say about it.

Everything is going to be fine.

I sit in the common room and listen to Muse's 'Origin of Symmetry' album on repeat and focus on my classics revision, trying to memorise some Latin vocab, getting Aled, my only friend in school today, to test me every now and then. I just need to stop thinking about it all. Everything's fine. I'm worrying about nothing.

After lunch, after I've failed for the third time to remember what 'latrocinium' means, Aled puts down my pack of cue cards and looks at me. Aled Last doesn't have a load of friends – he's extremely shy so not many people try to talk to him – but I'd say he and Tao were two of my best.

'Ugh, sorry,' I say immediately. 'Wow. I need to revise more. God.'

Aled blinks at me, and then glances out the window.

It's another intensely sunny day. I probably should have just stayed in bed with Nick this morning.

'Maybe we should stop revising now,' he says in his tiny voice. He chuckles and looks down at his own revision – more colourful maths cue cards. 'Not that I've been doing much anyway.'

'Haha, yeah, same.'

'You okay though?' he asks. 'I feel like you've been really down today.'

I pause, a little taken aback. 'Oh. Yeah. No. I'm fine.'

'Yeah?' He fiddles with his fingers and gives me a look.

'Yeah. I don't know. Nick's just talking a lot about uni, it's kind of . . . just makes me feel a bit crap . . . I don't know.' I groan and run a hand through my hair. 'That sounds so bad when I say it out loud.'

'No, you're allowed to feel things.' He smiles. 'I get it.'

'It's not really fair on him though; like, he has a right to be excited.'

'Maybe you should talk to him about it. You've already talked about long distance and stuff, right?'

'Yeah, we've talked about it . . . I just don't think he realises how much it's . . .' I don't really know how to finish my sentence. 'It'll make him feel so bad though.' I shake my head. 'I don't want him to stop being excited about it.'

'Well . . .' Aled struggles to find something to say. He looks down at his desk and fiddles with his cue cards. 'I don't think you've got anything to be worried about. I mean, you know, you're . . . you're Nick and Charlie. You're not going to break up . . . I don't think . . . I mean, even Elle and Tao aren't breaking up and you know what they're like.'

Tao's been going out with Elle Argent, a girl from Nick's year, for almost the same amount of time

Nick and I have been going out. They do seem to bicker a lot but it's usually about very trivial things such as opinions about movies.

'Yeah.'

Aled doesn't say anything else, so I stand up and say I'm going to the bathroom. But I don't go to the bathroom. I walk all the way down to the locker room, just so I can lean against a wall in a locker row and take out my phone and try and think of something to say to Nick, some way of telling him what I'm feeling. But there isn't any way to say it, not without making him feel guilty. And that's the last thing I want.

Instead, I load up my Tumblr inbox, just to see if there's anything interesting in there, but there are only a few new messages asking whether I've thought properly about how long distance works, about whether it's really worth the pain, about whether Nick's really not going to meet anyone else at university while I'm not with him all the time. I don't mean to let this stuff get to me, but it still does. I even feel myself start to well up a bit, so I exit the Tumblr app and delete it from my phone.

We're fine. Why am I getting upset about this now?

Nick

When Charlie slumps into my car at 3:15pm, I can tell something's up. I say hi but all I get is a tiny grumble in response, and as soon as he shuts the door he leans on the window and closes his eyes.

I stay still for a moment, waiting to see if he's going to say anything. But he doesn't. 'You okay?'

'Mm,' he says, unmoving.

'Bad day?'

'Mm.'

I drive off without pushing it. If he wants to talk

about it, he will. That's one thing I've learnt about Charlie. If you try and make him talk about stuff he doesn't want to talk about, there's even less of a chance he'll eventually tell you.

By the time we get to Charlie's house he seems a bit better, so I don't bring it up. But something's still kind of *off* with him. He sits at his laptop in intense silence while I'm catching up with his mum. He spends at least half an hour choosing what to wear for Harry's party, even though he wears the same jeans and checked shirts everywhere anyway. It takes him significantly longer than normal to eat dinner, which is always a sign he's stressed about something. In the car on the way to Harry's house, his knees bob up and down.

Maybe he's pissed off at me for some reason. I have no idea why he would be.

We park down the road and he walks a little way ahead of me and Tori, Charlie's sister, who we gave a lift to.

‘Have you argued?’ Tori asks. ‘Seems like he’s pissed off with you.’

‘Not that I know of. I don’t know what’s wrong.’

‘Hm.’ She doesn’t say anything else.

Harry Greene lives in a townhouse near the high street. His massive parties are pretty much the main reason he’s the most famous guy at Truham. We know that by eleven almost everyone will be in the basement dancing to some crappy dubstep remixes. By twelve, people will be throwing up in house-plant pots and on the pavement outside. By two, people will be asleep in corridors, breaking away into different rooms to mess around, and getting high in the garden.

Sure enough, Harry's got music blasting from the basement making the floor vibrate and there are people everywhere, mostly Truham sixth formers, but definitely a few Year 10s and 11s too, and people from the secondary school across town. I think we were all supposed to be in the garden, but it's started chucking it down with rain. So much for summer.

As soon as we're inside and Tori's gone off to find her friends, Charlie speed-walks towards the kitchen for drinks. The kitchen table, as expected, is covered in bottles and plastic cups, and once we reach it Charlie downs a vodka shot, and then another one. I think this might be the point where I need to actually say something.

I touch his arm. 'Hey.'

He looks at me and takes a sip of the vodka lemonade he just made. 'Hm?'

'You okay?'

He nods a little too enthusiastically. 'Yeah. Fine. Why?'

I shake my head. 'You just seem sort of on edge.'

He looks away again and pours a drop more vodka into his drink. 'Oh. Just . . . a bit stressed because of revision . . . just been in a bad mood today . . .'

This seems like a reasonable explanation, I guess. Then again, Charlie could lie for Britain – he lies to *loads* of people. He lied to people at school for months about his anorexia. He lies to his parents sometimes when he wants to go out somewhere with me but isn't sure they'd let him. He lies to Mr Shannon to avoid becoming unpopular with other students. To be fair, he hardly ever lies to me, but occasionally I can tell that he's saying something just because he doesn't want to bother me. I think this might be one of those times.

He takes another sip. His eyes dart around the room. 'Best Coast,' he says.

'What?'

'The music. It's Best Coast.'

I hadn't even clocked that there was music playing in here. I try to think of something to say but he beats me to it.

'We should get drunk.'

I chuckle. 'I'm driving.'

'Oh.'

'You get drunk.'

'I plan to.'

'D'you think we should actually socialise first?'

He pours a glass of lemonade and hands it to me. 'Mm, fine.' He steps close to me, so close I almost think he's going to go in for a kiss right here in front of the people chatting and drinking around us, but

instead he just gazes up at me beneath dark hair with icy eyes, smirking slightly, the tease of a dimple in one cheek, letting loose everything that made me physically attracted to him in the first place. I'm half confused and half extremely flustered.

'Nick,' he says, so low and quiet I probably wouldn't have heard it had I not been staring at his lips.

I let out a nervous laugh, feeling my cheeks getting hot, but don't really know what to say. We're not exactly averse to public displays of affection, but we're never like *this* when other people are around. What is he trying to do?

'I want a drunk hook-up in the bathroom later,' he murmurs, and then he walks off before I have the chance to answer him.

Charlie

I am aware that I am combatting my feelings about Nick going to university by a) refusing to talk about it and b) flirting with him so hard it's actually embarrassing, but honestly, I'm *this close* to punching the next person who even uses the word 'university' in a sentence. I have not punched anyone yet in my life, but it's never too late to start.

Oh, and c) I am getting drunk.

Very drunk.

It doesn't take a lot to get me drunk, which is

extremely useful for situations like this, where Year 13s are everywhere and no one will shut up about leaving school and prom and summer and university and I just want to go *home*.

I stay away from Nick as much as possible because hearing him talk about it is the worst part of all of it.

I am a terrible person.

It's eleven o'clock now and I've lost count of how many vodka-lemonades I've had, and I'm having to stay seated on an armchair next to Tao in the conservatory because standing up is proving quite difficult at the moment. There isn't really enough room for both of us on the armchair and my leg is sort of going numb because Tao is slightly sitting on it, but he's too engrossed in talking about something or other, I don't know, I'm not really paying attention—

'Have you and Nick talked about it?' he says, snapping me out of my daze, but it's still like I've got cotton wool in my ears and nothing that's happening is actually happening.

'What? I wasn't listening.'

Tao grins at me. He always seems more like his eccentric self when we're outside of school. Tonight he's wearing a stripy shirt that was probably intended for a businessman, with rolled-up green trousers and his signature red beanie. He genuinely does think he belongs in a Wes Anderson film.

He throws his arms around me and rests his head on mine. 'Aw, you're such an adorable lightweight. I'm glad we're not leaving school this year.'

'If one more person mentions leaving school, I'm literally going to cry.'

He pats my cheek. 'There, there. It'll all be fine. You're Nick and Charlie, aren't you?'

'I don't know what that means,' I say.

Nick

Everyone is talking about uni.

I don't think I've ever been so excited for something, or so *ready.* And everyone else going to uni seems to agree. It's the start of freedom. Doing things because we *choose* to do them. Finally being treated as *adults*.

But I get that, like, Charlie might not want to talk about it all the time. I mean, he's still got a year of school left.

But it gets to eleven and Charlie is definitely avoiding me. Normally we stick pretty close together at parties, and considering how he was acting earlier . . . well, I'm a bit confused, if I'm honest.

I find him curled up in an armchair with his friend, Tao. I say hi to Tao and exchange pleasantries but can see Charlie staring at me. I crouch down next to the armchair so our eyes are level. His are unfocused and he's blinking a lot – he's pissed, all right. 'You okay?'

'I'm *fine*,' he snaps, with an irritated grin. 'God, you don't need to, like, check up on me every second, Jesus Christ.'

I feel myself recoil. Charlie hasn't snapped at me like that for *months*. What the hell have I done?

I stand up again. 'All right. Fine. No need to shout at me.'

He looks away. 'I wasn't shouting.'

'Yeah.' I turn around and go to leave the conservatory, but not fast enough that I don't hear Tao say to Charlie, 'What's going on?'

Charlie

It's midnight and I'm in the basement, where almost everyone's come to dance, hoping that the blast of dubstep, some crappy remix of a Daft Punk song, will drown out the buzzing in my brain, but it doesn't. I can't stop thinking I'm a piece of shit, I'm the worst boyfriend in the entire universe. I lean against the wall but just end up sliding down it so I'm sitting on the floor, all the dancers blurring in front of me under Harry's flashing fairy lights. Why am I being so weird and angry? Why am I like this?

'Charlie!' shouts a voice over the music, not Nick's, and I look up and there's Aled, gazing down awkwardly in his burgundy jumper. He squats down next to me. 'Are you all right?'

I swallow, so close to saying no. No, I'm ridiculous, I'm hilariously un-all-right. 'Yeah, yeah, I'm fine.'

'You don't look all right.' Aled frowns. 'Did you . . . is this because of Elle and Tao?'

Maybe I'm just hallucinating conversations now, maybe my brain is just stringing random words together. 'What? What d'you mean?'

'I just thought . . . you know . . . what I said about Elle and Tao yesterday . . . like . . . it was stupid, I feel really bad . . .'

I shake my head, wanting to laugh. 'What the fuck are you talking about, Aled?'

'You know . . . Elle and Tao breaking up.'

I spring forward from the wall. '*What*?'

Aled's eyes widen. 'Oh, oh, God, I just assumed you would know by now. They just decided that they're breaking up at the end of summer, I just heard . . .'

I stare at him.

'*What?*'

Aled looks down. 'Yeah . . . Tao was just like, *yeah, we're gonna keep on going out until Elle leaves but we think long distance will be too hard.*'

'But, Tao didn't tell me . . . I was talking to him earlier . . . I don't . . .'

Aled says nothing.

I open my mouth to say something, but nothing comes out. Why would anyone just end a relationship because it's got to go long distance for a bit? Elle and Tao clearly like each other a lot. They pined over each other for *ages* before they started dating.

Why would anyone do that?

Nick and I aren't going to do that. Nick thinks long

distance will be fine. He doesn't want to break up with me.

Does he?

Does he want to break up with me?

'Oh God, Charlie, what's . . .' Aled's started speaking because I've started crying. Great.

'Sorry . . .' I say, but my voice definitely isn't audible above the deafening music and I'm not sure who I'm apologising to anyway. 'Sorry . . . I'm so sorry . . .'

Nick

Since I haven't seen Charlie for half an hour, I think now might be a good time to go looking for him again, even if he is in a mood with me. What is his *deal* though? He's actually starting to piss me off a bit now. I've done nothing for him to be in a mood with me about.

I find him in the basement and he's just sitting in a corner with his friend Aled, so I go over to him, hoping that his weird bad mood has gone away, but as I barge through the dancers, getting closer and closer, I start to realise that his cheeks are damp and he's been *crying*, and that's when I start to feel seriously concerned. Something's definitely wrong.

I kneel down next to him and Aled gives me this panicked look like he doesn't know what to do. Charlie rolls his head towards me and he's even drunker than earlier, if that's possible. No wonder he's sitting on the floor in the basement.

'What's wrong?' I shout over the music.

He laughs but it looks wrong, something is really wrong. 'Are you gonna start talking about university again?'

'What?'

'It's pissing me off so much, Nick.'

I squint at him and ask, 'Pissing you off?' but he just mumbles something in reply and I can't hear him properly.

Then he pulls me towards him with one arm and kisses me.

I quickly discover drunk kisses are not fun when one person is sober – I can feel the dampness of his cheeks and he tastes of alcohol. It takes a few seconds for me to actually realise what's happening and in that time, I blink and see Aled make a look of startled distress, stand up and walk away.

I gently push Charlie off me. 'No. You're drunk.'

'*Niiiick.*' Charlie tries to lean forward again but I just lean backwards.

'Charlie, you're acting really weird.'

'No, I'm not.'

'*Yes, you are.*' I pull him by the arm so we're both standing. He staggers and grabs on to my arm with both hands. 'Come on, let's go upstairs.'

He doesn't answer, so I lead him back through the dancers and back upstairs, where it's nearly empty now – almost everyone is dancing in the basement. I guide him to the conservatory which is, as I'd hoped, empty and quiet, apart from the rain that's pummelling against the glass roof.

I sit him down on the armchair again and crouch in front of him. 'What's going on?'

He doesn't look at me, or even seem to have heard me.

'*Char.*' I say this a little louder and this time he meets my eyes. 'Why are you acting like this?'

'What?' he snaps, shaking his head. 'What am I *acting like*?'

'Like one minute you're seriously pissed off with me and the next you want to get off with me!'

He bends over and puts his head in his hands. 'I feel sick.'

'For fuck's sake.' I stand up. This is hopeless. 'Why are you being such a *dick*?'

He doesn't move.

'Just talk to me!' I say.

He says nothing.

'You can't be angry at me if you can't even tell me what I'm doing wrong!'

He makes a groaning noise and shakes his head in his hands.

'Fucking *hell*,' I say, sitting down heavily on the sofa opposite. 'Well, I don't fucking know what to do then.'

'Stop shouting at me,' he mumbles from behind his hands.

'I'm not shouting at you!'

'You *are*.'

We sit in silence for a minute until a particularly loud thunder crash makes me jump. Charlie notices and raises his head.

'You can break up with me if you want,' he says.

It takes a few seconds to process that.

'What?' I say. I stand up again and feel myself *really* getting angry now. What is he *talking* about? Where the hell has this *come from*? 'What the *fuck* are you talking about?'

'If you . . . want a fresh start, or . . . something . . . if you think long distance is too hard . . .' His eyes are unfocused again, his words slurring. Lightning flashes overhead, brightening the room. Why is he saying these things?

'What? Is that what *you* want?' I huff out a laugh. This can't be happening. 'You want us to break up. Is that it?'

'I just . . . want you to be . . . happy . . .'

'Bullshit,' I spit out, my voice definitely too loud now.

'Elle and Tao are breaking up . . .'

'What, so we need to break up too? You're not even going to *try* to stay in a relationship with me?' Part of me wants to talk this out rationally, but most of me is just pure *anger* and I don't even know why. I think I'm just tired of all this. Tired of all this bullshit and all this university talk and remembering that I've only got a few months left with Charlie.

'Why are you saying these things, Charlie? If you're trying to break up with me, just fucking spit it out.'

But I don't want him to. I feel like I'm about to be sick.

Charlie just shakes his head and stares blankly at the space next to me.

'Is that why you've been acting like this?' I say. 'You want to break up with me, but you're not even fucking brave enough to say it? You want to force me to break up with you instead?'

He's crying again now, his head shaking from side to side and his knees bobbing up and down. But he doesn't say anything. He doesn't deny it.

'Well, fuck you then,' I say, and that's when I realise that I'm crying too. God, how long's it been since that happened?

And then he raises his head and full on shouts at me. 'Well, it's *me* who's getting left behind!' He points towards somewhere indeterminable outside and his voice breaks. 'You're fucking off to university where you'll meet loads of new people and it's me who's getting *left behind.* We keep being like, *oh, everything's going to be fine, we'll Facetime loads, blah blah blah*, but it's not going to be all right, is it?' He gestures wildly, his eyes darting around the room. 'It's *not* going to be all right, it's going to be *crap* for me. I'm going to be stuck in this shitty town all by myself, but here you are, talking about it like it's the fucking *best thing ever*, and you know what? It makes me feel like *shit.* It's like you're looking forward to getting rid of me, like you can't *wait* to finally get out of here and get away from me—'

'What the *fuck?!*' I shout back, running a hand

through my hair. 'What d'you want me to do?! *Not* go to university?'

'*No!*'

'Because that sounds like what you're saying.'

'I'm not—'

'You've got no *fucking right* to be annoyed with me about that. I'm a year older than you, I'm going to university in September. That's just the way it is.'

He stares at me, eyes wide and filled with tears, and then he looks down. 'Why are you being like this?'

'Mate, what the fuck am I *being* like?'

Charlie looks up again and when he moves his hand, his eyes are thin slits.

'Don't call me *mate*. You never call me *mate*.'

I just shake my head and let out a huff of exasperation. 'You really are being a proper dickhead tonight, aren't you?'

'*Just leave, then*!' he shouts. The rain falls harder than

ever – I can barely hear him over the noise. 'Fuck off, then!'

'Yeah, fine. No problem.'

And that's it. I walk out of the room.

Standing in the corridor is Tao Xu, who has probably heard every word. God, this is all his and Elle's fault. If they hadn't fucking broken up in the first place, Charlie wouldn't . . . he wouldn't want to . . . he wouldn't have thought he'd . . .

'Is he . . . are you okay?' Tao stutters.

'See what you've done?' I say, stepping past him. 'Fuck you.' He cowers back. I want to say something else to him, but I can't think of anything, my mind's gone blank, I'm still processing what's just happened. What *has* happened? Everything was fine yesterday. This can't be the end. This can't possibly be the end.

I barge through the people chatting and smiling and laughing in the living room until I'm out of the house and in the rain, and by the time I reach my car I'm soaked and shivering. I turn the engine on but I just end up sitting in my car for twenty minutes, maybe because I'm too scared to drive when I can still hear thunder in the distance, or maybe because I'm hoping Charlie's going to run out of the house and open the door and say that everything he'd said was a drunken mistake. But he doesn't. So I just sit there.

THREE

Charlie

I wake up because the sun is in my eyes – I forgot to close my curtains last night. I forgot to do a lot of things last night. Like be a decent human being.

I fumble for my phone before realising it's still in my back pocket, and I'm still in my clothes. It's quarter past ten in the morning. No texts, no Facebook messages, nothing. I don't want to get out of bed to change. I don't want to do anything.

I don't want to do anything.

Last night . . .

What was I even *thinking*?

The Elle and Tao thing freaked me out. That after all this time, they'd just be, like, 'Cool. Yeah. We're breaking up. Oh well.'

After *two years*. Didn't they . . . didn't they *love each other*?

No. I guess not.

And I guess I started to think, 'What if Nick's bored?'

We don't do many exciting things. We just sit around at each other's houses.

I'm pretty boring as a person.

So, I guess I wanted to test him, to check whether he wanted to break up, but I couldn't even *say* it. I couldn't even say it properly.

Stupid.

I'm stupid.

I'm a fucking stupid idiot.

I'd rather not have known. I'd rather have just

carried on in blissful ignorance of what he thought, rather than this absolute mess. Now I have no idea what he's thinking. Is he just angry at me, or does he actually want to break up?

The thought of texting him to find out makes me feel physically ill.

We've argued before, but nothing quite as bad as this. We've never woken up still angry at each other. I haven't woken up feeling this shit in a long time, hungover and wanting to be sick and wanting to cry and that familiar emptiness I thought I'd gotten rid of a long time ago. That feeling that makes me want to stay in bed and never get up again.

One time when I was in Year 11, a few weeks after I got out of the hospital, Nick said something he didn't mean while we were eating dinner – some stupid thing about how I wasn't trying hard enough – and I started having a go at him and it turned into a massive argument, ending with him leaving. But even then, he still came back a while later. And everything was okay again.

I roll over so I'm out of the sun and pull my covers over my head, but the birds tweeting outside are too loud and it's still too bright in my room, so I just end up lying there. I wish I could turn back time. I wish I could keep turning back time to Thursday, and every time I got to the end of Thursday, I'd rewind time to the beginning of Thursday again, and I'd just be with Nick every day for the rest of my life.

Can't believe I even think stuff like this. Pathetic. I'm so pathetic.

'Morning,' says my sister Tori when I slump down next to her on the lounge sofa. She's in her pyjamas and dressing gown and is watching *Bridesmaids* with a large bag of Kettle Chips on her lap.

'Morning. Why are you watching a film at eleven o'clock in the morning?'

'Why not?'

'Why Kettle Chips?'

'First day of study leave treat.'

'It's your second day of study leave.'

'Then . . . it's my second day of study leave treat.'

I laugh and watch the film with her for a few minutes. I never really got into this film, but Tori's weirdly obsessed with it. It might be because the main character is super sarcastic, just like her.

'So . . . you feeling okay?' She turns to me. 'Have you had breakfast?'

'Feel a bit sick. It's nearly lunchtime anyway.'

'Hm.' She doesn't comment. Normally Tori's the first one to make me eat when I don't want to. 'What happened to Nick last night? You're lucky Becky had her car. And why were you

drunk and crying in the conservatory?'

I groan and roll my head back against the sofa. 'Do we have to talk about it?'

She shrugs and looks back at the screen. 'Nope. Thought you might want to.'

We sit in silence for a minute.

And then I decide to tell her.

I tell her the full story, not that there's much to tell anyway. Nick constantly talking about university, me getting all anxious about it, hearing about Elle and Tao, getting scared, saying stuff I shouldn't have, Nick freaking out – everything is my fault, as usual.

'Jesus,' she says, once I've finished. She gazes at me, the remains of her eyeliner smeared under her eyes, and then she pauses the film. 'Sounds like a really bad argument.'

'Yeah, no shit.'

'You don't think he wants to break up, do you?'

'Well, I don't know. Maybe. He didn't say *no I don't want to break up*, you know? He just . . . got so angry . . .'

And then suddenly I feel tears in my eyes. I bring up a hand to cover my face and when I speak, my voice is all high-pitched and wobbly. 'I feel like shit.'

'Oh, Charlie.' Tori puts down her crisps and pulls me into a hug, running one hand over my back. 'It's okay.'

I shake my head into her shoulder, trying not to get tears all over her dressing gown. 'It's not okay . . . it's really not okay . . .'

She lets me cry into her shoulder for a few minutes before she speaks again.

'I think you need to talk to him.'

'I don't know what to say,' I whisper.

'Just something. Anything.'

'He hates me.'

'That's untrue.'

'He's angry.'

'That's temporary.'

'I don't know what to *say*.'

'It doesn't matter what you say,' she says. 'You just have to say something.'

Nick

Saturday is a nothing day. I get up at around ten. I take Henry and Nellie for a walk. I eat. I have a nap. I play with Henry in the living room. I play video games for five hours. I eat again. I nap again. I go on YouTube for four hours. I discover that I've lost my disposable camera. I spend an hour looking for it. And then I cry myself to sleep.

On Sunday morning I stay in bed. I start to realise that the reason I feel numb is because I'm in shock. In shock that Charlie would even suggest breaking up. I also start to realise that the shock is turning into panic, I'm panicking now, panicking that long distance really isn't going to work after all, that it's going to be too hard. If Charlie's this upset now, he'll be even worse when I leave. But I can't stay here just because he's upset about it. What am I supposed to do? There's nothing I can do. Nothing. It is what it is. Charlie wants to break up with me before it gets too painful. Maybe we'd end up breaking up anyway. Maybe we're just getting it out of the way.

What? I don't know. I have no idea what I think any more.

I go to text Charlie but then realise I can't because I don't know what to say. I can't speak to him until I actually understand what I feel.

I start crying again.

Mum asks me what's wrong on Sunday afternoon. I tell her me and Charlie had an argument.

'Oh, you two'll get that patched up though, won't you, love?' she says, and then leaves the kitchen before I have the chance to say: not necessarily. Maybe not. Maybe this is it.

Charlie

Wednesday arrives and I still haven't done anything and neither has Nick. I guess I hoped if I waited long enough, he'd be the one to text me first, or call me, or *something*. But there's nothing.

Honestly, I have no idea what he's thinking. Maybe he really *does* want to break up. Why else would he have just lost it at me? He's never been so angry with me before. God, I wouldn't blame him if he wanted to break up. I'm pathetic.

I try to distract myself with revision, but it doesn't

really work. My Thursday Latin language exam rolls around and it goes fine. I memorised all the vocab in the end; there's nothing I'll let stop me from doing my best in my exams. But I don't feel happy when it's over. I just check my phone for the six hundred billionth time. And there's nothing, of course. Nothing.

I know I should text him, but if I ask whether he really does want to break up and he says yes, I don't know what I'll do.

What's the point of a life without Nick?

Wow. I'm so embarrassing.

If he wants to talk to me, he will. If he doesn't then I guess that's it.

That's the end.

Nick

Nine days since the party. A Sunday. I messed up my psychology exam on Friday, but I don't think that was because of our argument. Everyone knows psychology A Level came straight out of hell.

I've got a few days until my next exam so I don't do anything again this weekend. I don't even take the dogs for a walk; I ask Mum to do it. I just sit in my room, curtains shut, playing video games, watching TV, doing nothing.

Mum walks in at around 1pm to ask if I want

lunch, but stops when she sees me wrapped up like a burrito in my duvet, my hair greasy and a property show on the TV.

She sits down on the bed. 'You all right, Nicky?'

'Mmm.'

'How's Charlie? I haven't seen him for ages.'

I blink slowly and look at her.

'We argued.'

'That was a while back though, wasn't it, love?'

'Nine days.'

'And you still haven't sorted it out?'

'No.'

'Oh, baby.' She pats what she thinks is my leg but is actually just a bit of lumpy duvet. 'Have you tried talking to him?'

'He broke up with me.'

'What? Are you sure? That doesn't sound like him.'

'Yes.'

She breathes out. 'Oh, baby. I'm so sorry.' She holds out her arms for a hug and I sort of fall into them, still in my duvet-burrito form. 'It'll be okay. You'll be all right.'

It takes quite a lot of effort not to start crying again.

'D'you want to order pizza tonight?' she asks. 'Special treat.'

I nod. 'Yes, please.'

'I love you so much, baby. You'll be okay.'

'Love you, Mum.'

But I don't think I'll be okay. Ever. I don't think I'll ever be okay ever again.

FOUR

Charlie

Two weeks after the argument is my penultimate exam – music. A Friday. I don't think about anything except my exams for the entire week. Well, except the fact that I can't remember the last time I spent two *days* away from Nick, let alone two entire weeks. God.

Do I need to start trying to get over this? Because I have no idea how people do that. Nick is the best and most important person I have ever met.

God.

I go out with my friends that evening, just to Simply Italian for a big end-of-exams celebration meal, even though my last exam isn't until next Thursday. I try to have fun and laugh at people's jokes and talk about how horrible exams were, but everything's fake. I don't want to laugh at anything. I want to go home and sit in bed and do nothing.

Tao's on my left. He's laughing and joking with the rest of our friends, but I can tell he's joining in to hide how sad he is about Elle. How did they decide to break up? Did they just agree it'd be for the best? Or did they have a big argument like me and Nick? I don't want to bring it up and upset Tao more.

On my right is Aled. He stays quiet for most of the evening, as he often does, but as we're all sorting out who's paying what, he says, 'Charlie,' and I look at him, and I see genuine concern in his eyes.

'Have you spoken to Nick at all?' he asks.

Word of our argument has spread everywhere, obviously.

'No,' I say, trying to keep any and all emotion out of my voice.

'So . . . is that it, then?' His voice is almost a whisper. 'Have you, erm, broken up?'

'Yeah.' I realise that this is the first time I've said it. I've been distracting myself up until this point, but now I don't have revision to distract me any more. And there it is. We've broken up. 'Yeah, I, erm . . . I think so.'

Aled looks at me for a long moment. 'I'm so sorry.'

'Not your fault.'

'No, but –' he shakes his head – 'you're Nick and Charlie.'

I laugh. 'What does that *mean*?'

'It's . . .' He laughs too, a nervous expulsion of air. 'You're . . . it's hard to explain. It's like, if you had to provide evidence for soul mates, everyone would pick you two.'

I snort. 'There's no such thing as soul mates.'

'Maybe. But you two present a pretty convincing argument.'

'If we were, he wouldn't have broken up with me.'

'Is that actually what happened?'

I stare at Aled. I've never heard him so assertive. I don't know how to answer.

'Did he actually say, *Charlie, I want to break up with you*?'

I frown. 'Well, no, not exactly. But, he didn't say *I don't want to break up*.'

'But obviously he wouldn't have said that.'

'What?'

'If he thought you were trying to break up with him, he's not going to start protesting against it. If he thought you didn't love him any more, he wouldn't make it difficult for you. He'd just be heartbroken.'

'Well, he's an idiot then!'

Aled laughs. 'Exactly. Two idiots in love. Couple goals.'

'Great. Thanks.'

Someone interrupts us to see whether Aled's sorted out what money he owes. I really want to believe what he's saying. That Nick never wanted to break up.

Maybe it's time to find out.

As soon as I get home, I sit down at the breakfast bar where Tori is sitting with her laptop and a large glass of diet lemonade. She turns to me.

'You look at least two hundred per cent more cheerful than you have been collectively in the past two weeks,' she says.

'I need to talk to Nick, like, *soon*.'

She throws her hands into the air. 'Jesus Christ! Finally! Revelation of the century!'

I swivel on the stool. 'But also, I really don't want to.'

'Yeah, yeah, yeah. You've had your tantrum time, okay? You're a Year 13 now.'

'Not till September.'

'I always count it from the last day of the year before.'

'Well, I don't.'

She takes a long sip of lemonade and then points violently at the door. 'Go talk to him, you giant child!'

'Oh my God, *fine*!'

I get up from the breakfast bar and wander towards the door, but Tori speaks just as I'm about to leave.

'By the way, I found this stuffed between the sofa cushions.' She picks up something next to her and holds out Nick's disposable camera. 'Is it yours?'

I take it from her. 'Oh, that's Nick's.'

'Oh. He might want it back then.'

'Yeah.' I walk slowly out of the room. The number on the tiny screen at the back is at zero – I didn't even know Nick had taken that many pictures. When did he take them all? He could only have left the camera here two weeks ago while we were getting ready for the party, and I didn't see him take any then. So it must have been the day before that.

And that's when I know exactly what I'm going to do.

★

Straight after my shift at the café on Saturday morning, I speed-walk to Boots to get the film developed.

I have absolutely no idea what's on it, but I figure there might be something I can send Nick. I don't know whether that'll help anything. But a picture speaks a thousand words, I guess. Blah blah blah, something cheesy and romantic. Yep. Cool.

I arrive at Boots and it turns out I have to wait an hour for them to develop the photos, so I wander around town with my umbrella over my head. I buy an Oreo Dairy Milk bar from a newsagent's because Nick's obsessed with them. Then I sit down on a bench and take out my phone, balancing my umbrella on my shoulder.

And then I see I have a text from Tao.

I open it immediately.

Tao Xu

(15:34) *Hey Charlie, I know the past few weeks have been kind of awful for both of us because of stuff with Elle and Nick but I wanted you to be the first to know that me and Elle are getting back together. We talked about it some more and we're both SHIT SCARED about being long distance . . . but deciding to break up was a mistake. We both still love each other so much haha. So we want to at least try to make it work!!*

My heart nearly thumps out of my chest. Tao and Elle made a mistake. They're *getting back together.*

Charlie Spring

(15:52) *omg. i'm so so happy for you, i know you two are good together*

Tao Xu

(15:54) *Also I'm so sorry if me and Elle caused some*

weird drama between you and Nick and I really hope it's cool between you guys soon, and if this is at all helpful I saw Nick quickly as he was leaving Harry's and he was really upset about it . . . like I'm pretty sure there's no way he wants to actually break up with you.

I read the message several times before replying.

Charlie Spring

(15:58) *it's definitely not your fault . . . i'll keep you updated. i don't really want to break up either haha*

And that sort of makes me feel a bit better. Just saying it out loud.

I do not want to break up with Nick.

After that, I wander back to Boots to pick up the photos.

I don't look at them until I'm on the bus home.

The first photo is the one Nick took of me when I found him in the box fort on the last day of school. I look sort of bewildered. My eyes are all wide and my mouth half open, and it's not a *terrible* photo. It's nice because it looks natural, I guess.

The second is the one Harry took when we weren't looking, and it doesn't look half as awkward as I thought it was going to. We're standing on the grass with our hands touching, just sort of looking at each other like we've come to a pause in conversation, the grass at our feet and the trees overhead looking so bright in the sun. It's kind of arty. Harry would probably be very pleased with himself.

The third is the one I took of Nick, and it *is* a terrible photo. I laugh out loud. It's hilarious actually – he's mid-blink. He'll probably throw it in the bin as soon as he sees it.

And the fourth one is the selfie we took together,

Nick's arm around my shoulders and our heads together, both of us smiling, a little lens flare from the sunshine falling across Nick's chest. I look at that one for a while. That Thursday was such a lovely day. I wish the past two weeks had been as lovely as that day.

There are a few after that still at school, several of Nick with his Year 13 friends and even a couple just of the school building itself, as if Nick just wants to remember what it looks like.

And then there's the one of me in Nick's car. Sitting with my legs tucked up on the seat, my sunglasses on, scrolling through my phone. It's nice. I hardly ever see pictures of me like this; they're almost always selfies or posed photos with friends.

The bus jolts suddenly and the photos fall off my lap on to the seat next to me. I slam my hand down on them before they fall on the floor but they've all spread out like playing cards, and one photo catches my eye.

It's me, asleep in Nick's bed. The streetlights outside send a soft orange glow through the thin curtains behind me. My hand is curled next to my face and my hair has gone all messy and pushed to one side. I don't know when he took this one. I think I fell asleep before him but I honestly can't remember.

Maybe it's kind of a weird picture to take, but I can understand why Nick took it. I'd take a picture of him if he looked like that in my bed. God, that sounds creepy, doesn't it? I don't care.

As I flick through the rest of the photos, I start to realise that they're all sort of like that, all tinged purple and blue and orange, muted colours, a little blurry, like polaroids at an art-school exhibition.

Me stretched out on his bed on his laptop. Me lying on the lounge floor with my arms around his border

collie, Nellie. Me attempting to give his pug, Henry, a piggyback. Me several steps ahead in the field behind his house when we took the dogs for a walk. Me standing at the top of a hill, holding out my arms – I remember him taking that one. Me giving him side-eye as I caught him trying to take a picture of me against the view, the sunlit horizon and the fields and the river. A selfie of us together. A selfie of us with me holding Henry up so he could be in it too. A selfie of us making stupid faces. Back at his house, a blurred close-up of me laughing from when he'd thrust the camera at my face. The light gets darker, bluer, a photo of me curled up on the lounge sofa, the TV screen illuminating the tips of my hair. Me cross-legged on his bed in just my T-shirt and boxers, pointing at the camera, smiling. And then the one of me asleep.

There are so many of just me.

Me.

Nick just took a ton of photos of me.

Nick's not a hugely creative person. He's never been interested in photography or art or anything like that.

I think he just took them because he wanted to remember what this was like. What our life is like now. Chilling round each other's houses, going on walks, eating together, sleeping together.

It sounds boring but it's so wonderful.

It is. I feel myself tear up just looking at our life together.

I love this. I love us. I love our weird, boring life.

I take my phone out of my pocket and take a picture of our stupid-face selfie in the field. I send it to Nick.

Nick

My mate Sai has come round to stage an intervention. He's going to Cambridge Uni in the autumn so I'm not entirely surprised that he's smart enough to pick up on the fact that I am approximately seventy miles away from okay, but he hasn't said anything useful so far and now we're playing Mario Kart and eating Percy Pigs.

After we've been gaming for around half an hour and chatting casually about A Level revision and summer and how utterly shit Harry's party was, Sai finally says, 'So what exactly are you both having an argy-bargy about?' He puts the controller down, swivels round on the sofa and folds his arms. 'Because it sounds like nothing, to be honest.'

I sigh and pause the game. 'Charlie broke up with me, mate.'

'Oh, *come on*. Why the *bloody hell* would he do that?'

'I have no idea.'

'Are you sure that's what he was trying to do?'

'Honestly, I'm not even sure. He was so drunk. He just kept telling me I should break up with him. And I just lost it at him.'

Sai adjusts his glasses and runs a hand through his hair. 'Sounds like you need to have a chat with him, dude.'

'I don't know what to say.' I put my controller down and look at him. 'Help me.'

'Why am I the relationship expert? I've never even been in a relationship.'

'You're smart. You're doing English Lit at uni.'

'English Lit is utterly useless in the real world, Nicholas. *Utterly useless*. Trust me. Chaucer and John Donne aren't going to help you with this.'

This makes me laugh. 'I don't even know who they are.'

'*Exactly*.'

I lean my head back on the sofa. 'I think he . . . just . . . thought it was a good time to end our relationship. Like, teenage relationships never last. It's a bit weird that we've made it this far anyway. And . . . I dunno, I guess he thinks we're kind of boring; like, we hardly do anything interesting. We're the most basic teenage relationship.'

'Basic teenage relationship?' Sai splutters. 'Have you seen yourselves? You hang around with each other every single day and somehow haven't wanted to kill each other yet. You've started sleeping round each other's houses regularly on *school nights*!? You can communicate by just *looking* at each other! Trust me, I've played board games with you two.' He shakes his head. 'A basic teenage relationship is daring to hold hands outside the school gate and going on cinema-and-Nando's dates on Saturday afternoons.'

I stare at him.

'If you want to break up,' he says, pointing a finger at me, 'go right ahead. If you're bored and want it to be over, fine. But just because you're not going on fucking amazing dates every weekend doesn't mean you're *boring* and definitely doesn't mean you need to break up.'

He slaps his hands on his legs and leans back.

'Shit,' I say.

When I pick up my phone a couple of hours later, I have a message.

The name on the screen reads **Charlie Spring**.

FIVE

Charlie

I send him another picture two hours later. The one of us kissing that I took on my phone.

Two hours after that, I send him a third picture. The selfie we took in school on his last day.

The next morning, an old selfie of us I find on my Tumblr.

Half an hour later, one of our first selfies, back when we started going out.

And I carry on like that until Monday. Picture after picture until I've sent every single selfie of us I have saved on my phone.

The little 'Read' tick appears on all of them until around Sunday afternoon. Then he stops reading them.

And he says nothing. He doesn't reply.

As soon as Tori gets home from her exam on Monday, I tell her all about it.

'He's not replying,' I say. It's actually embarrassing how panicked I sound. 'What does that mean?'

She stands at the door, not even taking her shoes off.

'You got those photos?' she says.

'In my room.'

'Go get them.'

'Why?'

'We're posting them through his letterbox.'

'Why will that help?'

'Because texts are dumb.' She shrugs. 'And a gesture is needed.'

I laugh. 'Who are you?'

'A born-again woman. Willing to put aside my

apathy for the sake of romance.' She blinks and puts her hand on her heart. 'Jesus, I gave myself indigestion saying that out loud.'

Tori's friend Becky drives us. Becky keeps looking at me in the rear-view mirror. I've never been truly sure whether Becky likes me or not, but right now, I don't think it matters.

It only takes a minute to drive there, but Tori says we have to drive because a quick getaway will be vital to the success of the 'gesture'. Sitting in the back seat, I flick through the photos again. Should I post all of them through the letterbox? Just a few? Just one?

I make the decision and take a pen out of my pocket.

Nick

I get home from my Monday afternoon exam, dump my bag on the floor in the hallway and fall on to the living room sofa. It didn't go too badly today. Only two more to go, and then that's it. Summer.

Summer. What am I going to do with all that time?

I almost don't want my exams to end now.

Charlie started sending me blank texts on Saturday while Sai was round. I don't really know what they're supposed to mean. My phone's quite old and I dropped it down the stairs a couple of months ago so I assume it's a glitch. I haven't turned it on since yesterday afternoon. Seeing Charlie's name keep popping up was making my stomach lurch every single time.

'Nicky? Is that you, love?' My mum calls from the kitchen.

'Yeah,' I shout.

'You've got post.'

I groan and rise from the sofa. I stumble towards the kitchen and walk towards the table, where there's a brown envelope with the word 'Nick' on it, no address.

It's in Charlie's handwriting.

And my stomach lurches harder than it has done all weekend.

'Oh my God,' I say.

'What's up?' Mum brings two mugs of tea over to the table and sits down, looking at me expectantly.

'It's from Charlie.'

Mum gapes. We both stare at the envelope for a long moment.

'Well, open it then!'

And I do.

Inside the envelope is a photograph – the sort you get developed from disposable cameras. And I know immediately that I took this one. I remember the exact moment I decided to take it, walking into my room after getting a glass of water to find Charlie curled up so beautifully in my bed, the orange street-lamp light shining on his skin, and I felt like if I was going to die, this would be what I wanted to see last.

I turn the photo over and there's Charlie's handwriting.

Hey. You take a lot of pictures of me. D'you have a crush on me or something? How embarrassing. If you wanna talk, I'll be at the Truham Primary School Summer Fete tomorrow (Tuesday) at 3 o'clock . . . wow this isn't a rom-com lol. I'm sorry for how sappy this is. Btw I love you. Ok bye xxxx

Nick
TEAR

Charlie

I haven't felt this nervous since I had to do my bloody Head Boy campaign speech in front of the entire school.

What if Nick didn't even see the photo? What if it, like, slipped underneath the doormat? Or his mum threw it away by accident? What if he saw the photo, tore it up, and didn't even notice the note on the back?

What if he read it and still doesn't turn up?

I arrive at Truham Primary School's Summer Fete, which takes place every year on their school field, with Tori and our dad at around two o'clock. We spend most of the following hour wandering round with our younger brother, Oliver, who's in Year 4 at the school. Dad gives him money to do the tombola and play on the bouncy castle and the coconut shy. Tori plays against him on the table football they've got set up in the middle of the field, and I mainly stand there, repeatedly checking my phone and searching around for my boyfriend. Ex-boyfriend? No. Not ex. Not yet.

I'm not giving up yet.

At quarter to three I go and wait near the entrance to the field, just inside the tennis court. It reminds me too much of the Truham tennis court, the day when all this had started, all these stupid, pointless feelings.

Charlie Spring

(14:54) i'm in the tennis court!! if ur coming

He doesn't text me back. It doesn't even say he's read the message. I feel myself start to sweat a little. Is this it? Am I going to give up after this? Am I going to be able to give up?

What am I going to say to him? Am I just going to beg him not to break up with me?

What if he turns up and still says he wants to break up?

I take a deep breath.

This is it, I guess.

I look up and watch as Nick walks through the tennis-court gate.

Having not seen him for over two weeks, just the sight of him makes me want to run up to him and kiss him and hold him and not let go of him for at least twenty minutes. I clench my fists and stay very still as he walks up to me. God, everything about him is so perfect.

'Hi,' I say as he stops and leans against the tennis court fence in front of me. I try to think of something else to say, but nothing comes to mind except 'you are beautiful' and 'I love you'.

'Hi,' he says, with a nervous smile.

There's a pause.

'I got the photo,' he says, and then shakes his head. 'Well, duh. Here I am.'

I huff out a laugh. 'Genuinely the most embarrassing thing I have ever done.'

'And you call *me* embarrassing.'

'That photo was pretty embarrassing, though.'

'True. We're actually both pathetic.' He grins and I feel a pang of hope.

'You didn't text me back,' I say.

Nick just blinks and says, 'You were just sending me blank texts. I thought it was a glitch or something.' He pulls his phone out of his pocket and shows me his messages. There's the one I sent him five minutes ago, and then there's just blank message after blank message.

Oh.

Right.

'Why, what did they say?' Nick looks at me curiously.

'Oh . . . I was, erm . . . sending you all the pictures, like, one-by-one . . .' I run a hand through my hair. 'That's so awkward. Wow. Sorry.'

'Pictures of us, you mean?'

'Haha . . . yeah . . .'

'I don't think this phone can get picture messages any more.'

I stare at him. 'Can't it?'

'Don't think so. You know I dropped it down the stairs it a couple of months ago? It's been doing some weird things since then.'

I shake my head, amazed. 'I knew you'd dropped it but I didn't know about the photo thing.'

He shrugs. 'Neither did I.'

'Oh.'

'Can I see them now?'

He's not laughing at me. He's serious. He doesn't think this was stupid.

'Yeah.' I take my phone out of my pocket and we scroll through the pictures one-by-one, laughing at the stupid ones and pausing on the cute ones. Occasionally we get to one that reminds us of an old day out and we stop and talk about it and remember, remember the silly dates we've been on and the terrible ones and the great ones, the repetitive days we spend indoors and outdoors, at school and at home. By the end, we're both sitting on the asphalt with our backs against the fence, the sun shining off the court and the white of our shoes.

We sit in silence for a minute, and then he says, his voice so quiet I only just catch it over the buzz of the crowd behind us, 'I don't want to break up with you.'

And I could honestly cry right there. I could just cry with relief.

'Me neither,' I say. 'Sorry if I sounded like I did. I really didn't.'

'Same.' He chuckles. 'I have no idea what we were arguing about.'

'Me neither.'

'Sorry I shouted at you. And didn't drive you home.'

'Sorry I got drunk and made out with you in front of everyone. And cried.'

'Sorry I called you a dick.'

'Sorry I told you to leave.'

'Sorry for talking about uni all the time.'

'Sorry for getting pissed off with you talking about uni all the time.'

He laughs, an amazing, boyish, Nick laugh. He rolls his head on to my shoulder. 'Can we stop now?'

I find his hand and take it in mine. I lean against him and he still smells like him. Like home. 'Yeah.'

'I don't want to break up with you, ever,' he says.

'Same.'

'Maybe that's stupid.'

'I don't care,' I say.

'Me neither,' he says.

He tilts his head up again and kisses me and I haven't felt like this happy for weeks, months, maybe ever, and something is different too, something I can't quite place. He brings a hand up to my cheek and I don't think things have gone back to normal – instead,

we've entered an entirely new era, one where we're better, surer, stronger together.

Wow. I really am embarrassing.

'Also, I bought you chocolate,' I say, when we break apart after a while. I take the Oreo Dairy Milk bar out of my pocket, hoping it hasn't melted too much in the heat.

'Oh man.' He grabs it and tears it open. 'That's it. You've sealed the deal now. We're practically married.' He pops a chunk into his mouth and then holds it out to me. 'Want some?'

I stare at the chocolate and feel that jolt of fear that I always get, but something, for some reason in that moment, makes me say, 'Yeah, okay.'

Nick

We decide to ditch the fete. Oliver will be fine with Tori and their dad, and there isn't really much for us two to do there anyway. We decide the beach is a much better idea.

It's about an hour's drive to the beach we always go to, so Charlie connects my phone to the car radio and plays some Sufjan Stevens, then Shura, then Khalid. There are closer beaches, but they're always busy and disgusting, packed with loud teenagers and toddlers and people fighting for a spot to lay their towel.

Our beach is a lot smaller. It has a thin pier you can walk down with a bench at the end, and a massive arcade just across the road that stays open until 10pm. There never seems to be many people on the beach itself, apart from a few dog-walkers and elderly folk, and it's no different today. It's just open space and flat blue sea and a beautiful horizon, as if the whole world had been made just for us.

We walk up and down the beach, talking, and we walk up the pier and sit on the bench at the end and talk and kiss, and then we get the rug I keep in my car and find a spot on the beach to sit down and then lie down and just be silent for a while.

We walk to the fish-and-chip shop we always go to and sit on the brick wall outside and eat and talk, and then we decide taking off our shoes and socks and rolling up our jeans and paddling in the sea is a good idea but quickly learn, once our jeans get wet, that it probably wasn't a very good idea after all.

We take a bunch of photos on Charlie's phone after talking about how he doesn't take enough. We go to the arcade for an hour and play on all our favourites: air hockey, the jungle car game, the skiing game, the basketball game, the coin machines. We get enough tickets for a bouncy ball.

We sit at the end of the pier again and watch the sunset, because that's what you've got to do on days like this. The clouds turn pink and purple, the sky orange, and then everything is dark blue.

On the drive back, Charlie falls asleep in my car. I turn the radio on and thank the universe that my life is like this.

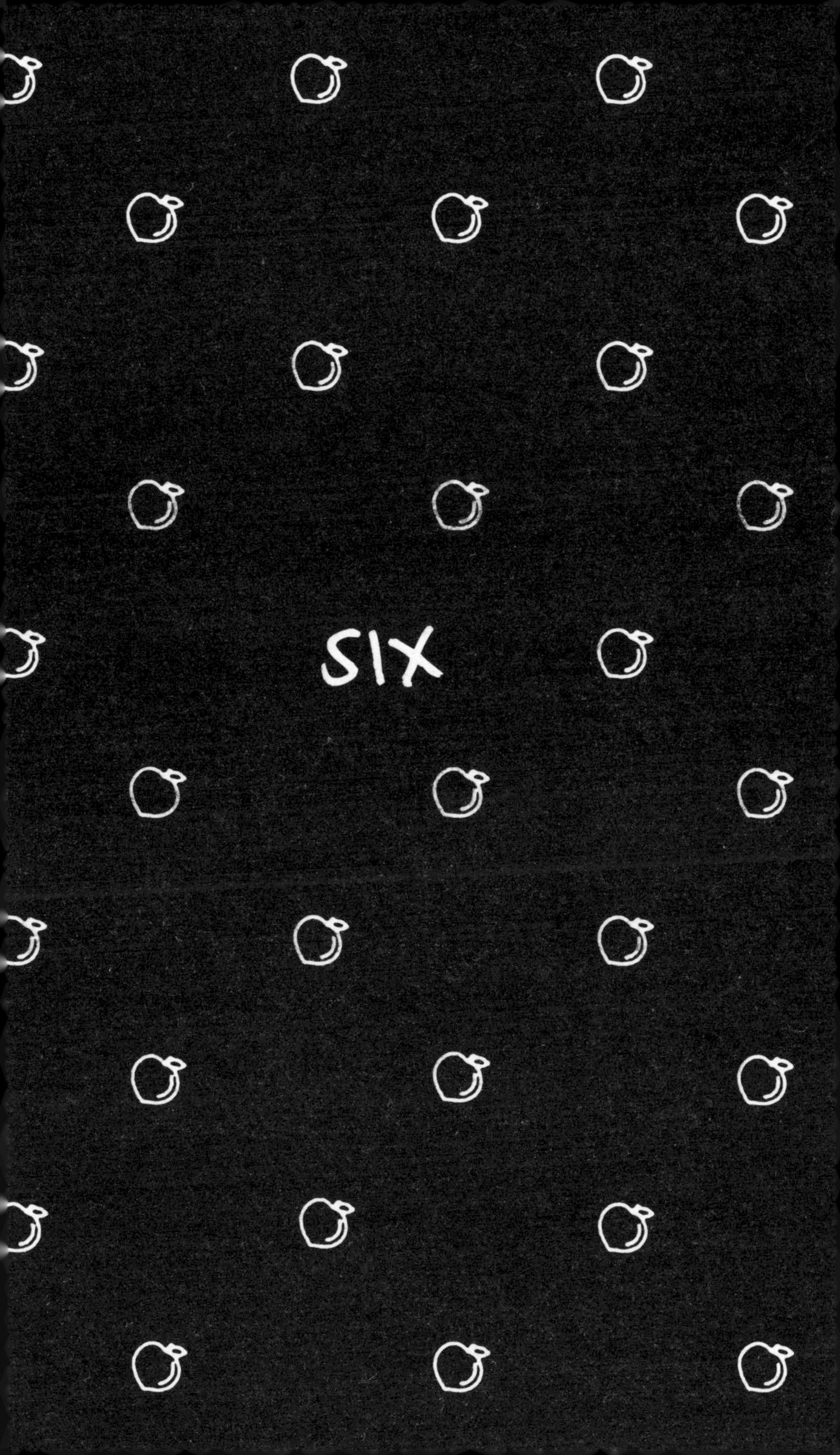
SIX

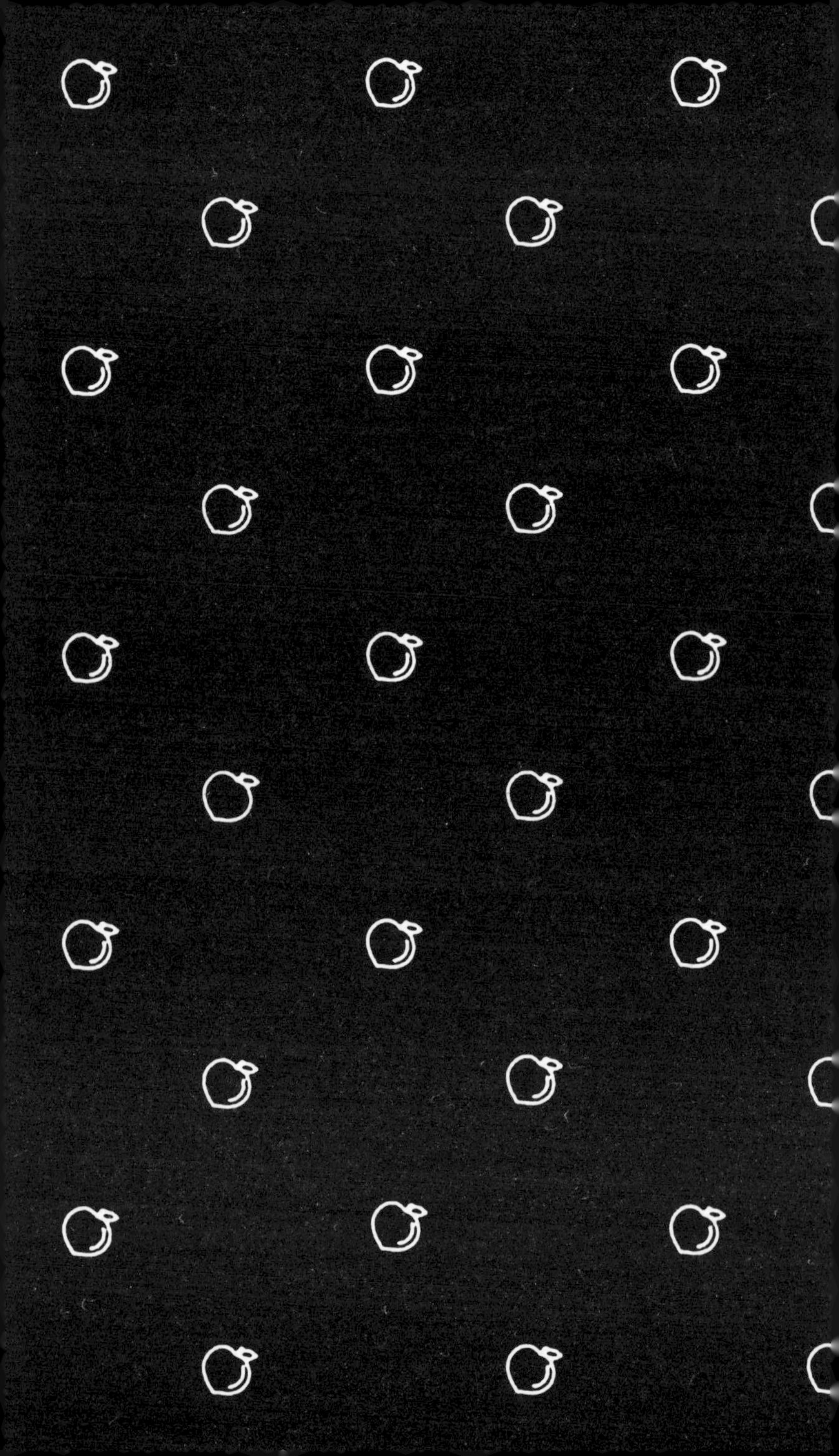

Charlie

Aled was right. Nick and I are literally two idiots.

We spend the whole day talking about us and what it's going to be like when we're long distance and it honestly only makes me believe even harder that we're going to be fine, that everything's going to be okay.

Everything is going to be okay. Seriously, this time.

Nick drives me back home, but I tell him to drive to his house instead. I text Tori that I'm staying over his. She'll explain to our parents.

We stay up late just talking and browsing the

Internet and watching videos and talking again, laughing, dozing off. I wonder what it'd be like to have a whole life of this. I think it'd be pretty great. Not gonna lie.

And then one minute we're lying there and the next we're kissing, and it's not like this is anything particularly new, but it *feels* new. It feels like we've been forced apart for a century and this is our reunion, a mix of relief and desperation, both of us clinging to each other on his bed, and when Nick breaks away to kiss my neck I just stop thinking entirely.

How is it that this still makes me so . . . How have two years gone by and I still feel like this in his arms?

We kiss for a long time, like it's two years ago and we're on Nick's lounge sofa trying to watch a film. Impossible. I can't think about anything else when he's running his hands so gently through my hair, across my back, over my hips. I ask if we should take our clothes off and he's saying yes before I've even finished my sentence, and then he's pulling my T-shirt off and laughing when I can't undo his shirt buttons, he's undoing my belt, I'm reaching into his bedside drawer for a condom, we're kissing again, we're rolling over – obviously you can see where this is going.

I don't know if it's because we're feeling especially emotional, or we're just tired, or these past couple of weeks have been too much, but this time reminds me so much of the first time we had sex.

We were both fucking *terrified*, and the whole thing was kind of terrible because we didn't know what we were doing. But it was good too, so good, because we were a mess of emotions and we were scared and excited and everything felt *new*.

So, this sort of feels like that.

Nick touches me like he's scared that any minute

I could disintegrate forever. When we're finally undressed completely he just stops and stares like he's trying to memorise every second of this. When we're moving he keeps saying my name over and over until I find it too ridiculous and tell him to shut up, but he just grins and keeps on saying it anyway, whispering it against my skin just to make me laugh. I hold him so tight against me, as if that'll keep us here, keep him here with me.

I used to think I was pathetic for thinking soppy, romantic stuff like that. I don't any more. I just keep thinking it. I keep wanting him here. I keep wanting him to stay.

Afterwards we lie there for a while, Nick's head on my chest and our legs entwined. I reach over to his bedside table and turn the radio on, noticing that it's gone 3am – how did that happen? I close my eyes because I think Nick might be asleep, but several

minutes later I hear a click and open my eyes to find he's taken a photo of us lying there, this time on his phone.

'*Nick*!' I grab his phone and check the photo as he laughs gleefully.

'Nothing like a post-sex candid.'

I don't reply because I'm just staring at the photo – it's like the ones he took on his disposable camera, natural and un-staged, Nick curled against me and smirking up at the camera, my head leaning on his, my eyes shut and mouth slightly open.

'Don't delete it,' says Nick.

'I'm not.' I look at it for a second more, and then hand it back to him. 'Don't put it on Instagram.'

'Can I set it as my wallpaper?'

'What, and get rid of Henry and Nellie? Do you finally love me more than your dogs?'

'Mmm, that's going a bit far . . .'

I roll over, shoving him off me and flipping us so I'm lying on top of him. 'Rude.'

Nick laughs and wraps his arms around me. 'Okay, fine, I love you more than my dogs.'

'Good.'

'I love you more than anyone, actually.'

He says this a little quieter. I move my head out from the crook of his neck so I can meet his eyes.

'Is that weird?' he continues, and then huffs out a small laugh. 'I'm only eighteen.'

'I don't know,' I say. 'Maybe.'

It is weird. We both know it's weird. We both know *we're* weird, we're not like other couples our age. It's weird that we hang out every single day, it's weird that we'd rather just be with each other all the time. Every day we wonder when we're going to stop feeling like this and get over our teenage relationship. But it never happens. We just keep on going.

Because it's good too. God, it's *so* good.

'I'm weird too,' I say, because saying 'I love you more than anyone too' back to him doesn't feel quite adequate, even though I honestly love him more than anyone else in the entire world.

Nick squeezes me and says, 'Yeah,' because he already knows.

Nick

The next morning I wake up to the sound of Charlie's phone alarm and he makes honestly the most adorable grumbling sound I've ever heard and even though I'm half-asleep I just start laughing. He turns the alarm off and rolls over and asks, 'What?' and I'm like, 'Don't go to school today. You don't have to go to school . . . it's study leave . . .' And I reach out my arms and pull him closer to me and he shuts his eyes and mumbles, 'Fine.'

?
..♡
KISS
KISS

Nick Nelson

FULL NAME

Nicholas Nelson

AGE

18

SCHOOL YEAR

Year 13

BIRTHDAY

September 4th

LIKES

- rugby
- dogs
- baking

DISLIKES

- horror movies
- bugs
- bullies

Charlie Spring

FULL NAME

Charles Francis Spring

AGE

17

SCHOOL YEAR

Year 12

BIRTHDAY

April 27th

LIKES

- music
- Nick's hoodies
- naps

DISLIKES

- no wifi
- being cold
- bad mental health days

Read on for exclusive bonus material . . .

First day

07:31am

good morning! rise and shine! it's the first day of the rest of your life etc!!

Good morning!!!! I miss you soooo much

nicholas it's literally your first day of university. i saw you YESTERDAY

And???

I'm just being honest

Bearing my heart and soul and stuff

i miss you too you loser

what's on the agenda today

Got a 'welcome to Leeds' presentation at the student union this morning, then the freshers fair this afternoon. And I wanna properly meet my flatmates at some point

Actually I think I hear someone in the kitchen right now

omg go say hi

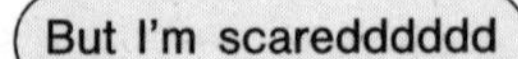
But I'm scareddddd

nick

they're gonna love you

you're gonna make lots of new cool friends and you can tell them all about me

i will be the mysterious sexy boyfriend of nick nelson, spoken of with reverence, like a myth passed down generations

then when i come visit you can introduce me to all of them and they will all be like wow... charlie spring we've heard SO much about you, you're so sexy and mysterious

You've really thought about that haven't you

it's been one of my semi-regular daydreams yes

Okay I'm going

i can't wait to hear all about it!!!

I love you mysterious sexy boyfriend

i love you too

dork

12:42pm

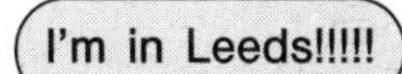

yes i am aware

No I mean I'm in the city centre wandering around 

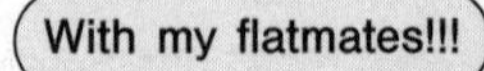

 omg!!! what are they all like?

They're all nice 

There's this girl Chloe who's really chatty and friendly, she's kinda posh, like she grew up in a giant countryside house with horses and stuff. Then another girl Jade who's American and maybe a bit shy, but she's sweet 

Then two guys - Miles who is gay and from London, he's kinda loud too, he and Chloe are sort of automatically the leaders of our flat haha 

And the second guy is called Laurence but he didn't really wanna hang with us I don't think so I don't know where he went 

 miles is gay! a new gay friend!

Haha yeah!! I haven't mentioned I'm bi yet tho, hard to find a moment to just like say it 

 it's okay

it'll come out when you're drunk and crying about how much you miss me

when that happens i want a video of it btw. or a drunk voice note at the very least

Don't because I will actually do that

i can't wait

Miles and Chloe were talking about going out tonight

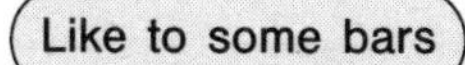

Like to some bars

d'you wanna go?

Yeah!! I mean I guess I haven't really done that before so I don't really know what to expect

Not like there's anywhere much to go in Truham lol

It sounded like Miles and Chloe have been out a lot already, Miles was saying he had a fake ID in school

well this is the university experience!!!
bars and clubs and parties

and if you hate it you can just go home

I feel like that's your life motto

it is

We're gonna get lunch in the market now I think

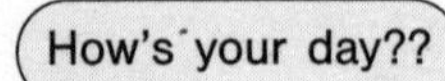

very normal and boring haha just school!

go have fun with your new friends!
i'm so glad they're nice

tell me all about it later

xxxxxxxxxxx

16:11pm

Char I have so much to tell you

Just went to the freshers fair with my flatmates

And like one of the first stalls was the LGBT+ society

please tell me you joined!!!

Well Miles was like 'I need to join' and then Jade was like 'hey me too, I'm bi!' and they walked up to the stall. And then I kind of followed them
and I wasn't really saying anything and after they wrote their names down I did too. And they were just looking at me and it was kind of awkward

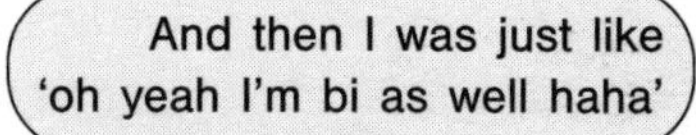

nick!!!! proud of you

i assume they were very chill about it?

Well kinda? Chloe and Jade were definitely. But like Miles was VERY surprised

And then when he kind of wouldn't stop talking about how he'd never have guessed I was bi and like I don't seem queer at all

that's a bit shitty

No it's okay, like I get it

I don't really look queer

I mean I know queer people can look like anything but like I don't have the queer signifiers. Miles said my Nike sweatshirt is very straight ahaha

nick any queer person who actually knows you can tell that you're queer, i promise

Wait really haha??

there's just an energy that queer people have and you have it. it's hard to explain but sometimes you just FEEL IT, it's like a sixth sense

anyway this miles boy shouldn't be making such a big deal of it

It's okay, tbh he's the sort of person who just says whatever they're thinking

well i'm proud of you for joining the lgbt+ soc!!! i bet you'll make even more friends there

did you find the rugby club too?

Yeah!! OMG so you know when I came to the open day and I met that queer rugby player?? He was running the stall!!!! He was so nice and he remembered me!!

awwwwww!!!

Tryouts are on Thursday

It's pretty competitive but there are lots of different squads so hopefully I'll get in somewhere

you def will

Anyway I'd better go, I need to go to Tesco

what thrilling plans you have

Hey I'm gonna be partying into the night actually

you are and i can't wait for the drunk photos

11:27pm

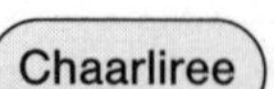

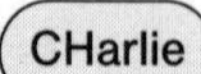

I thing I drank to much

nick

are you drunk

Me Miles Chloe and jade went to a bar and then another bar and now were in a club

Something bad happened!!!

something bad??? what happened???

nick!! are you okay?

please just reply saying you're okay

I'm okay dw!!! Just awry

*awkward

do you wanna facetime? or call?

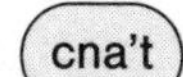

Still in the club

I so awkward lolllllll

can you tell me what happened?
i'm worried about you

message me when you can

11:58pm

hey, how are you doing? all okay?

00:43am

nick? i'm really worried here, i'm not gonna be able to sleep until you let me know you're not dead in a ditch

nick????

nick are you okay??? please just reply something if you're okay!!

Hiya, this is Nick's flatmate Laurence, just letting you know he's all good, quite pissed but he'll be fine! I'm just walking back to our flat with him now, I'll get him some water and tucked into bed haha

omg thank you!

sorry, hi, i'm just his worried boyfriend haha

I gathered, Nick won't stop talking about how much he misses you and how soft your hair is

01:45am

Omg these messages

How am I gonna face Laurence ever again

hello!!

I've downed like a litre of water and I feel much less drunk now

I'm in bed in my pjs

oh my god i want to hug you

wish i was there so bad

I wish you were here

In my new bed

It needs christening

when i visit we can make that happen xx

Charlie I'm having very sexy thoughts but I'm too tired to do anything about it

okay okay let's talk about something else

are you okay? you said something bad happened?

Oh shit yeah

Ugh

Yeah something kind of shitty happened

oh nick... do you wanna talk about it?

Yeah I mean it's not a huge deal. Just kind of shit

So everything was kind of fine for a bit. Miles and Chloe had a couple of bars they wanted to go to so we had a few rounds there, and they brought along a few new friends they'd made as well so there was quite a big group of people

I was trying to pace myself because I didn't wanna be like off my face in front of all these new people but Miles was really doing the most to get me to drink, buying me shots and being like 'aww don't be boring' when I said no

fucking dick

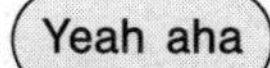

Yeah aha

Well by the time we got to the club I was already quite drunk I guess. Me and Jade had been chatting a lot, she's really nice and she's really into basketball so we were talking about sports a lot haha. So I was mostly sticking with her

But we got separated in the club and I ended up with Miles and some of his mates and I was feeling a bit awkward because honestly they're not really my sort of crowd. So I just kept drinking more

nick :(

And then I realised Miles was like really trying to get with me

ah i thought that might be the case

Obv I was like 'I have a boyfriend' and was really trying to get him to leave me alone but he was very persistent, he kept touching me a lot

wish i'd been there

would have cussed him out

would have kicked his ass

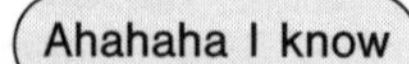

I was too awkward and trying to be polite when I prob should have just told him to fuck off

Like he literally went in for a kiss and I had to just step backwards and away

That was after I told him I had a boyfriend

oh i hate him

Anyway that's kind of it. It kind of threw me and then I went off on my own but couldn't really figure out where I was because I was so pissed

fucking hell nick i want to hug you SO BAD

your flatmate Laurence messaged me, he seemed nice?? he said he walked you home

Oh yeah!! Yeah so I was just kind of on my own in the club lol and then suddenly Laurence appeared and I was like 'hey I know you' lol

He'd been out with some guys from his course, he does maths so he must be smart

And he's actually really nice, he said he was thinking about heading back anyway and we should walk together

I talked about you the whole way home

I was literally ranting about how much I miss you all the way home

I wanna die

god i love you

Laurence seems really chill, I'm gonna talk to him tomorrow and say thank you

sorry miles turned out to be a prick

I guess I was excited at the thought of having some new gay friends here but yeah

you've got jade! a bi buddy!

Yeah!!! She seems much more like my sort of person. And so does Laurence, I mean idk if he's queer but he seems chill

dyou wanna sleep now?

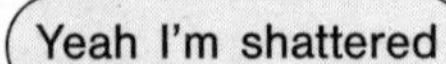

First night at uni... bit of a mess

there will be MUCH better nights, i'm sure of it

something was bound to go wrong today.
it's your first day

but you'll find your people and you'll figure out what bars and clubs you like and what ones you hate. and you'll become a uni rugby star and you'll get better at telling people to fuck off and sometimes you'll get too pissed but you'll have mates with you who'll look after you and get you home. and you can tell me all about it

I love you

nick i love you so much

so fucking much

Thank you for listening to my nervous rambles today

i love your nervous rambles. music to my ears

go to sleep and we'll talk more tomorrow

I love knowing we have tomorrow

always

God we're so embarrassing

terribly embarrassing yes

wouldn't have it any other way

Sleep well char xxx

good night xxxxxxx

About Alice Oseman

Alice Oseman was born in 1994 in Kent, England. She completed a degree in English at Durham University in 2016 and is currently a full-time writer and illustrator. Alice can usually be found staring aimlessly at computer screens, questioning the meaninglessness of existence, or doing anything and everything to avoid getting an office job. Alice's first book, SOLITAIRE, was published when she was nineteen.

Follow Alice Oseman on Twitter and Instagram (@AliceOseman)

Fall in love with
Nick and Charlie
in another novella:

This Winter

A HEARTSTOPPER NOVELLA
THIS WINTER
ALICE OSEMAN
BESTSELLING AUTHOR OF HEARTSTOPPER AND LOVELESS